T0381986

For Tilly and Archie xx – L.R.

For Theia-Louise, Phoebe-Rose
and Isabella Grace xxx – K.H.

Lucy Rowland  Katy Halford

There's No Such Thing As...
DRAGONS

SCHOLASTIC

"There's **no such thing** as **dragons,**"
my grandpa said last night.

Today I'll go **exploring**

just to see if he is right.

I've packed my **Dragon Facts** book . . .

but there's **such** a lot to do!

And so much **searching** to be done so
could YOU help me too?

There's **no such thing** as **dragons**.

I know they like their lairs.

I checked all round my secret den

(it's underneath our stairs).

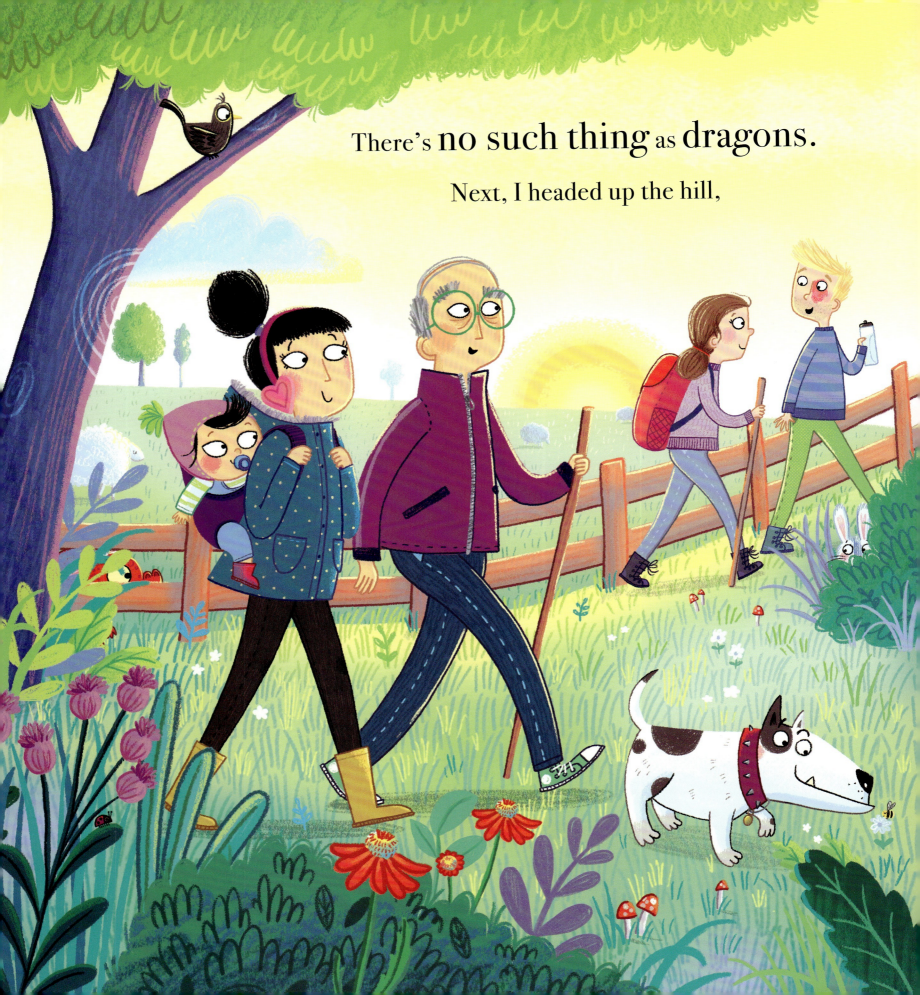

There's **no such thing** as **dragons**.

Next, I headed up the hill,

but if they're up here hiding

then they're keeping very still.

There's **no such thing** as dragons.
I thought they might live higher?

I clambered up the mountain next,

but saw no smoke or fire.

There's **no such thing** as dragons.

I tried the forest too.

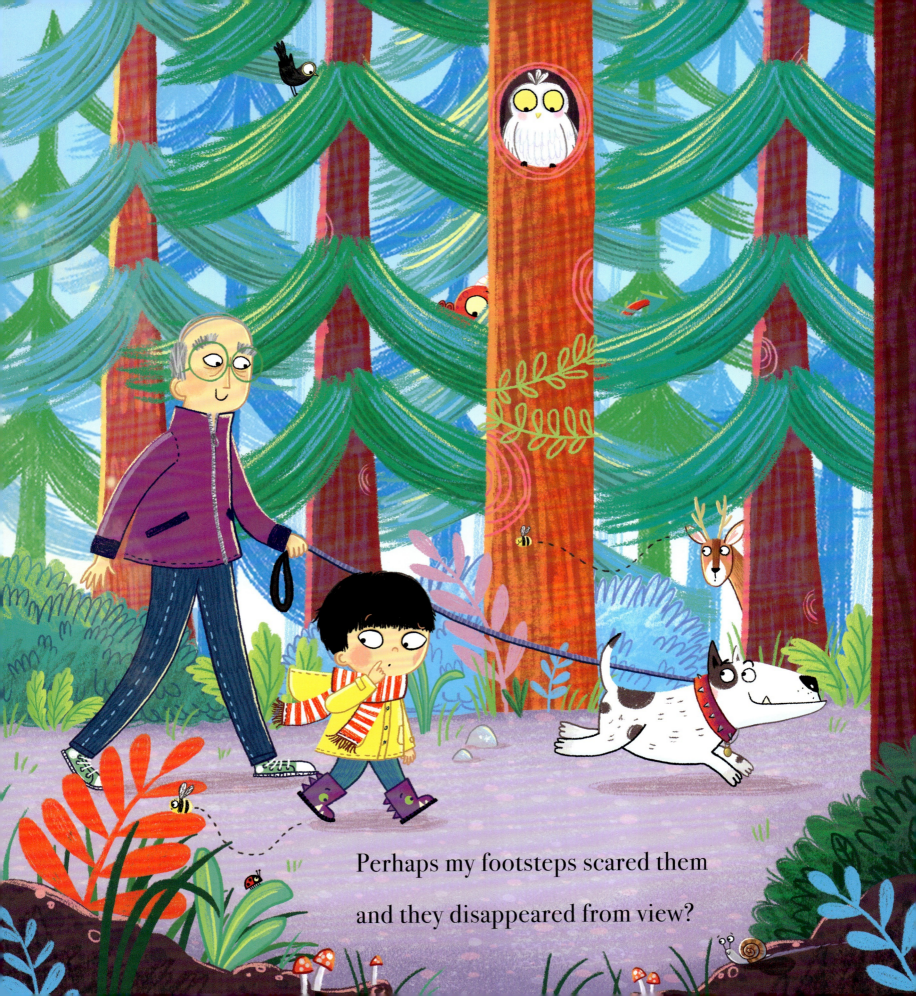

Perhaps my footsteps scared them

and they disappeared from view?

There's **no such thing** as dragons.
but I know they like to fly.

Hot air balloons and aeroplanes

were all that I could spy!

There's **no such thing** as **dragons**.

The museum in the town
had lots of big, old dinosaurs . . .

DINOSAUR EGG
·1·8·5·9·

DIPLODOCUS

Tiny head

Bulky body

8m Long neck

Adult human to scale

Five feet

FOSSILS

no dragons were around.

There's **no such thing** as dragons.

See, I even tried the zoo!

CAUTION
MONKEYS

The monkey thought he'd seen one
(but he doesn't have a clue)!

MONKEYS
- TERRIFIC TAILS
- LIKES TREES
- DIET: NUTS, SEEDS, BUDS, FLOWERS, INSECTS

NO FEEDING!

There's **no such thing** as **dragons**.

Nope! I scaled the castle wall.

I found some knights in armour
but no dragons there at all!

There's **no such thing** as **dragons.**

Only one place left to look.

But no – no dragons by the rocks . . .
except inside my book.

"Oh, there you are!" my grandpa calls.

"I've looked all round for you!"

"There's **no such thing** as **dragons**," I explain.
"It must be TRUE."

He holds me very tightly
and I hug him tight as well.

We watch the shadows dancing

and it's almost like a spell.

Then, as we turn to leave the cave,

some smoke – it fills the air.

A rustle! Then the cave turns warm . . .

A DRAGON,

standing there!

My grandpa laughs. His eyes are wide.
He thinks we've got it wrong, but . . .

there ARE such things as dragons,
and I knew it all along.

Published in the UK by Scholastic, 2023
1 London Bridge, London, SE1 9BG
Scholastic Ireland, 89E Lagan Road, Dublin Industrial Estate,
Glasnevin, Dublin, D11 HP5F

SCHOLASTIC and associated logos are trademarks and/or
registered trademarks of Scholastic Inc.

ISBN 978 0702 30223 7

A CIP catalogue record for this book is available from the British Library.

Printed in China
Paper made from wood grown in sustainable forests and other controlled sources.

3 5 7 9 10 8 6 4

This is a work of fiction. Names, characters, places, incidents and dialogues are products
of the author's imagination or are used fictitiously. Any resemblance to actual people,
living or dead, events or locales is entirely coincidental.

www.scholastic.co.uk

MIX
Paper | Supporting
responsible forestry
FSC® C008047